Another book about bears.

Once upon a time, in a deep, dark forest, far, far away, there lived an old brown bear.

One day, the bear embarked
upon a magical

Oh, no! No! No! No! Hold it right there! Not another book about bears!

enchanted and
behold th   ious Esquilax.

Before   he brown bear
had wan   he woods
where the   face with
the hand   ale.

The   ppeared
to be   the   f the rare,
a horse with   f a rabbit,
and the body   it.

Err, bear, you're kind of interrupting my story. What's the problem?

Do you know how many books have been written about us? I'll tell you ... too many!

Whenever you open up a book about a bear, we have to perform the story for you ...

CHILD OPENS BOOK

BEAR ALARM SOUNDS

BEAR PERFORMS STORY

BEAR ZONkED

Even if we were in the middle of something really good – like sleeping, snoozing or napping – we have to jump up and do whatever the book says.

Why do you like reading about bears so much?

We're not so great.

We're often greedy ... grumpy ...

lazy ... and a bit ferocious.

And we're exhausted! We are sick of
doing all the work.

I see. But who will the children read about?

You can't quit!

We can. And we just did.

Hmmm, we'll see about that.

The bear wore a pink tutu and rode a tiny bicycle ...

Oh, I see. You'll make us look silly if we don't cooperate? Well, it won't work.

He chowed down on piping hot porridge.

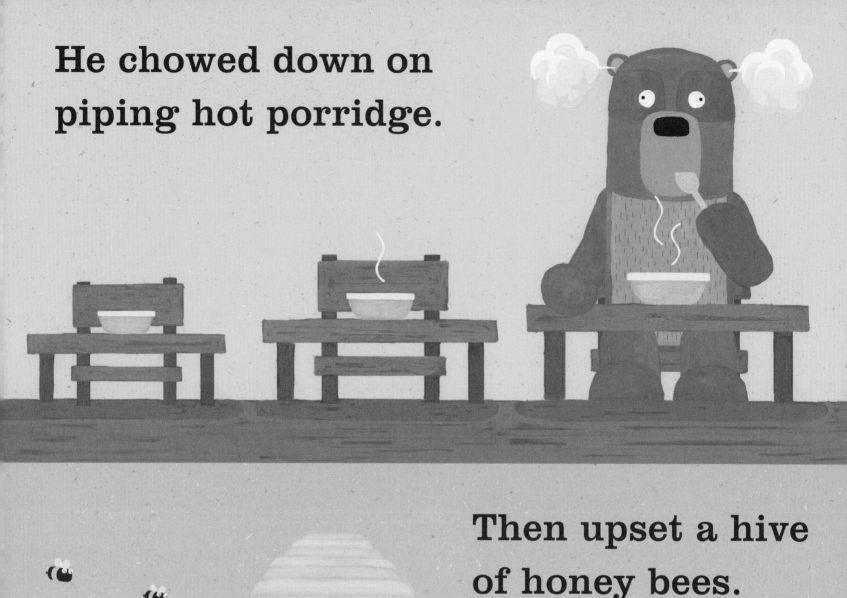

Then upset a hive of honey bees.

Buzz off!

And turned a frog into a handsome prince with a big, sloppy kiss.

The children cried and cried when their favourite character turned out to be a big, selfish meanie.

Oh, that's low.
Fine, how about this ...
if I can find a better
animal to star in your
books, you'll leave
us alone. No more
books about bears.
Deal?

OK. Deal.

Meet your new leading animal!

Um, bear, do you know
how many elephants
you can fit into
one tiny book?
Not many.
They're too big.

OK, how about an echidna?
Hmmm, too spiky.

Kitten?
Too cute.

Crow?
Too noisy.

Star-nosed mole?
Too ... woah!

Flying fox?
Too batty.

Dodo?
Too extinct.

Crab?
Too pinchy.

Horse?
Neigh.

Peacock?
Too fancy.

Koala?
Too cuddly.

Earthworm?
Too boring.

Anglerfish?
Too ugly!

Kangaroo?
Too jumpy.

Salmon?
Hey, who took the salmon?

Cheetah?
Too fast.

Tortoise?
Too slow.

Gazelle?
Too scaredy.

Spider?
Too scary!

Blobfish?
Seriously?

That's all I've got. They're all the animals I know.

Well, don't you see, bear? No other animal has quite what it takes to star in all those good books.

Sure, bears are a bit greedy, grumpy, lazy, and even ferocious sometimes, but who isn't?

The fact is ... bears are just right.

So, what now?

Don't worry.
I have an idea.

Once upon a time, in a deep, dark forest, far, far away, there lived an old brown bear.

One day, the bear fell asleep and hibernated, uninterrupted, for eight long months.

Luckily, a few old friends agreed to help out while the bear took a well-deserved break.

The end.